# Calvin Coconut

## EXTRA FAMOUS

# Other Books About Calvin Coconut

# CalViN CoCoNut
# EXTRA FAMOUS

## Graham Salisbury

### illustrated by
### Jacqueline Rogers

## A yearling Book

All rights reserved. Published in the United States by Yearling, an imprint of Random House Children's Books, a division of Random House LLC, a Penguin Random House Company, New York. Originally published in hardcover in the United States by Wendy Lamb Books, an imprint of Random House Children's Books, New York, in 2013.

Yearling and the jumping horse design are registered trademarks of Random House LLC.

Visit us on the Web! randomhouse.com/kids

Educators and librarians, for a variety of teaching tools, visit us at RHTeachersLibrarians.com

The Library of Congress has cataloged the hardcover edition of this work as follows:
Salisbury, Graham.
Calvin Coconut : extra famous / by Graham Salisbury ; illustrated by Jacqueline Rogers.
— 1st ed.
p. cm.
Summary: Calvin and his friends have the opportunity to earn some money by appearing as extras in a zombie movie being filmed on a nearby beach.
ISBN 978-0-385-74220-7 (hc) – ISBN 978-0-375-99047-2 (lib. bdg.)
ISBN 978-0-307-97427-3 (ebook)  [1. Interpersonal relations–Fiction. 2. Motion pictures–Production and direction–Fiction. 3. Family life–Hawaii–Fiction. 4. Hawaii–Fiction.]
I. Rogers, Jacqueline, ill. II. Title. III. Title: Extra famous.
PZ7.S15225Cacm 2013
[Fic]–dc23
2012017513

ISBN 978-0-307-93075-0 (pbk.)

Printed in the United States of America

10 9 8 7 6 5 4 3 2

First Yearling Edition 2014

Random House Children's Books supports the First Amendment and celebrates the right to read.

For Olive:
Love to live. Live to love.
And dance, always.
And for my movie-making friends,
Dana Hankins and Tim Savage.

—G.S.

For Pablo

—J.R.

# 1

# Déjà Vu

It was Saturday morning. High above, the sun was an egg yolk sizzling in a big old Hawaiian-sky frying pan. I was sitting on the grass in my friend Julio's front yard, dreaming of a new bike.

Mine was too small now, and it didn't have gears. Riding that thing uphill set my legs on fire, and it was getting so I could hardly keep up with Julio and Willy, who had bigger, newer bikes.

My bike was embarrassing. It had fat tires and looked like something an old man would ride down a dirt road in a cow pasture . . . wearing a straw hat . . . with one pant leg rolled up.

For sure, I needed a new one.

Metallic red, or midnight black.

But who had money for fancy bikes? Not me.

I was jarred out of my daydream when Julio shouted, "Go *away!*"

Not at me, at his brothers.

We were waiting for Julio's mom to get back from the grocery store.

Julio's dad was at work, like always, and Julio was babysitting his four younger brothers . . . or the pests, as he called them. Right now they were running around us, yelling, zipping in, zipping out, trying to touch us as they passed by.

Julio covered his head with his hands. "Please! Make them go away!"

I laughed.

"It's not funny. How would you like to grow up in a zoo?"

Julio was my best friend. We'd been in the same class at school since kindergarten. I knew him inside and out, and I was used to him complaining about his brothers.

But this time he really seemed mad.

"I can't *stand* them! All they want to do is mess up my life. I'm serious! Please! Send them to the Humane Society. No! Send *me,* so some nice family can rescue me."

3

"Good idea. You do kind of look like a dog."

I cracked up.

"Shuddup." He shoved me.

"Okay, I'll help you. Let's see. I need a new bike and you need . . . what?"

"New brothers."

"They're not so bad," I said. "They just want you to play with them."

He gave me a look that said, You want me to run over you with a steamroller or an airplane?

I put my hands up. "Just saying they're—"

"Pests!"

Julio clammed up.

He yanked up hunks of grass in his fist and tossed them at my feet.

When Julio's mom finally came home, the brothers ran over and grabbed at the grocery bags. "Ice cream! Ice cream!" they all shouted.

"Thanks for babysitting, Julio," she said. "You can go play now."

"Play?" he said. "*Play?* Like what? I'm a little kid, like them?"

"My, my, aren't we testy," she said.

Julio turned away. "Aw, forget it."

His mom herded the brothers into the house.

"What's up?" I asked. "You're really being weird today."

"It's boring."

I nodded. "True. Listen . . . you hear ants snoring?"

Julio humphed.

My dog, Streak, who'd been sniffing around in Mrs. Costello's yard, trotted over to us.

She licked my hand.

"You're bored, too, huh?" I rubbed her head. "What do you know that we don't, girl?"

She sighed and plopped down be-side me. But her ears were perked up like somebody was coming.

I looked up the street. Nope.

"I know," Julio said. "Let's

go to your house and look for money in your couch."

"Are you kidding? Stella's home."

Stella—who wasn't my sister but lived with us to help Mom—was in a bad mood because Mom had to work, so Stella had to stay home to watch my little sister, Darci.

"What's wrong with Stella?" Julio asked.

"Same thing that's wrong with black widows."

Julio laughed.

I tapped Julio's arm when I saw this kid heading toward us, walking right down the middle of the street. It was like in the movies, some guy coming toward you with heat waves shimmering over the road.

The kid was wearing mirror sunglasses that flashed in the sun, and he had a way of walking that told you he had the whole world in his pocket.

"I don't believe it," I said. "Benny Obi."

Benny was a weird kid who'd moved to Kailua from the Big Island. He was in our fourth-grade class at school for a few wild weeks. Then he disappeared.

"I thought he was long gone," Julio said. "After what Tito did to him."

Tito was a sixthgrade bully who liked to embarrass people, make them look bad so he could look good.

Which was what he'd done to Benny.

And Benny vanished. Never came back to school.

"I know kung fu," Julio said, low.

I coughed up a laugh.

*I know kung fu* was Benny's famous line. It was the first thing he said to our class when Mrs. Leonard, the principal, introduced him to us.

Benny got even weirder. He turned out to be a bug eater, a cave crawler, a skull finder, and a spooky storyteller, and he didn't know beans about kung fu. He made stuff up left and right and you mostly couldn't believe a word he said.

Still, we liked Benny. He gave us more excitement during his few weeks at Kailua El than any of us had seen that whole year. He wore black T-shirts, army camouflage pants, those mirror sunglasses, and a red-eyed silver skull on a chain around his neck.

And we followed him around like puppies, just to see what he'd do or say next.

Now he was walking toward us with a grin.

He lifted his chin, Hey.

We lifted ours back.

Streak watched him, ears up, tongue limp in the morning heat.

Benny Obi had a strange kind of power. You looked at yourself in his mirror sunglasses and wanted to climb in there and see what was on the other side. He was like a magnet that almost *made* you stick with him whether you wanted to or not.

Mom called it charisma.

I didn't know that word, but I was glad to see him.

"Déjà vu," I said, low.

Julio laughed. "Hang on to your brain, or that fool will mess with it."

"Hey, Benny's all right, why you calling him a fool?"

"Just is."

"Dudes," Benny said, walking up. "S'up?"

"Selling my little brothers," Julio said. "Whatchoo doing here? I thought you moved back to Hilo."

"Hilo? Why you thought that?"

"Well, you never came back to school."

"Pshh. That's because I got in Iolani."

That perked me up. "You go to *Iolani*?"

Iolani was a private school on the other side of the island. You couldn't be an idiot and get in there.

Benny shrugged.

"Wow," I said. "I didn't know you were smart."

He took off his glasses and squinted at me.

"Uh, I mean . . . it's not easy . . . you know, that school."

Benny grinned and put his mirror shades back on. "Relax. I know what you mean. Hey, you guys ever been in a movie?"

"What kind?" I said. "Like a real one?"

"Of course a real one. You ever been in one? Because I have. A zombie one. And I'm going to be in another one."

"Hunh?" Julio said.

Benny nodded. "Yeah, it's called *Zombie Zumba.* It's gonna be awesome. Me and my uncle wrote it. He lives in Hollywood and is a millionaire. He also wrote *The People They Ate* and *My Cousin Is a Teenage Vambie*. Those movies made him rich and now he's got agents, movie stars, directors, and producers calling him up all the time looking for scripts. He has to turn them down, of course, because it takes time to write a good story. But this new one is so good we saved it for ourselves. He's going to be the producer, director, and all-around main boss of it, and he wants me to be in it because I can act. I was in *My Cousin Is a Teenage Vambie,* you saw that one?"

Julio laughed. "What the heck is a vambie?"

"It's a cross between a vampire and a zombie."

"Pshh."

"Vambie," I said. "Suck the blood, then eat the brain. Cool."

"We're going to

film the new one right here at the beach." He lifted his chin toward the ocean. "We're auditioning extras right now."

"Ho," I whispered.

Benny took his glasses off again and looked us over, smiling with his eyes.

"What?" Julio said.

"You punks want to be in it?"

# 2

# That Girl

"Of *course* we want to be in it!" I said. "We can act. Right, Julio?"

"Calvin. Listen to me. He didn't write anything. There's no movie. He's just talking."

Benny opened his hands. "Okay, if you don't want—"

"No-no," I said. "We believe you. Come

on, Julio! He's not lying. So, how do we do it, Benny? How do we get in the movie?"

Benny grinned. "Through me, of course. If I tell my uncle you'd be good, that's all he needs to know. He says I got a knack for making movies, just like he does. He says I come from that same special planet all good moviemakers come from. I got creative talent, and that's something you can't learn. You got it or you don't."

Julio grinned. "You come from a special planet, all right."

Benny nodded. "Yeah, I like that. I don't want to be like everyone else."

Julio snorted. "Don't worry."

"Thanks," Benny said, serious. "And there's more. If you get in the movie, you get paid."

I banged Julio's arm. "Paid!"

The Movie Planet

Julio raised an eyebrow. "How much?"

Benny thought. "Hundred dollars."

"A hundred dollars!" I said, picturing that shiny new bike. "Holy bazooks!"

Benny nodded. "Yeah, hundred."

Julio's other eyebrow went up. "I could use it to buy a ticket to a place with no brothers."

"So," I said. "What do we do?"

"I got a part you'd both be perfect at: zombies."

Julio looked at Benny. "Zombies?"

"You got the look."

I cracked up. Julio's bad mood was perfect. He did have the look.

"Tell me you're not making this up, Benny," I said.

"It's real as your dog."

I looked at Streak, now snoring. Benny and Julio thought that was hilarious.

"Fine," Julio said. "Anything to get me

away from here. Might as well be in a fake movie that only exists in Benny's head." He stood up.

Benny raised a hand. "Not so fast. We need girls, too. Know any who can act?"

I tapped my chin, thinking.

"There's Maya from our class. Remember? She lives over there." I pointed up the street. "She'd be good. And we could get Shayla. I know where she lives, and she can dance, too."

"Zombies don't dance, they stagger. But in this movie they do sort of move around like dancing. Yeah, she would be good. What about older? We need a teenager to run along the beach for a beach runner part . . . human, not zombie."

Stella came to mind. No, no, no, I thought.

I tried to chase her name away.

No luck.

It was painful, but you gotta do what you gotta do if you want to be in a zombie movie.

"Uh, there's this girl who lives with us.

She's in high school. I don't know if she can act, but she's really good at being mean."

Benny smiled. "Mean sounds good. Someone who doesn't take no for an answer. Where is she? I'll know if she's right when I see her. All she has to do is say a few lines. If she looks good, I can teach her to act. Uncle said I could talk a button off a shirt, and he's right, because I got the gift."

"What gift?" I said.

"Kung fu," Julio mumbled.

"Shhh," I said. "Benny, what gift?"

"Talk. If you can talk, you can do anything. That's what Uncle said."

Julio slapped his leg. "Well, if talking is talent, you got more talent than anyone on this whole planet."

"Hey, I can't help it." Benny looked hurt.

I jumped in front of Julio before he ruined everything. "You're right, Benny. You got talent, so let's go see that girl. If she's too mean I bet you could turn her around like that."

I snapped my fingers.

Benny pointed at me. "Watch me work."

Stella was standing out in the yard keeping an eye on Darci and her friend Reena while they played near the river that ran by our house.

"Stella!" I called.

She ignored me.

Julio stopped in the street and glared back at his house. His brothers were out in the yard again, and they wanted to follow us.

"Don't!" Julio made a fist.

I pulled him along.

"Stella," I called again as we walked up.

She turned and squinted, shading her eyes from the sun. Her mouth was puckered like a prune.

"Uh, this is Benny," I said. "He wants to meet you. His uncle is making a movie, and Benny is looking for girls . . . I mean, actors who are girls . . . teenage girls, like you."

Stella turned from me to Benny.

She waited.

Benny cleared his throat and ducked his head. "Uh, yeah, uh . . ."

Julio laughed. He was scared of Stella, so he loved seeing someone else cower at her stare.

Stella looked at Julio and he shut up.

I said, "Benny wants me and Julio to be in the movie, too, right, Benny?"

Benny swallowed, digging up his courage.

"Uh, yeah . . . and . . . well, my uncle is the director and he needs a girl, uh, an actress."

Stella crossed her arms.

Down at the river, Darci and Reena were looking up at us.

"Yeah," Benny said. "So . . . you want to try out? Can you act?"

Stella sliced me up with her razor-blade eyes. "Is this some kind of joke, Stump? If it is, it's not funny."

"No," I said. "It's for real. And don't call me Stump."

Stella turned back to Benny. "What is it, a commercial for shampoo or something? A school project?"

"No, my uncle is a famous Hollywood screenwriter and a millionaire. He wrote big hit movies, like *The People They Ate* and *My Cousin Is a Teenage Vambie*. You saw those?"

Stella turned back to me. "It is a joke, isn't it? You're trying to be funny. Well, how about this—beat it! You little boys go play somewhere else. I don't have time for this dumb game."

"No," I said. "Benny's uncle is—"

Benny snapped his fingers. "Perfect! I like your attitude. For the part I'm thinking about you're a natural. I can tell because I have a nose for it, Uncle said."

Stella made a fist and knocked on Benny's forehead. "Hello-o. Is anyone in there? I said beat it."

Benny let her knock on his head, grinning. "Yeah . . . you'd be perfect. Say some lines for me. Here. I'll give you um."

He reached into his pocket for a folded piece of paper.

Stella put her hand up. "Stop!"

Benny froze.

"Okay," Stella said. "Say for the sake of amusement this isn't a joke. What kind of movie is this?"

"A zombie one," Benny said.

"Zombie."

"*Zombie Zumba*. That's the title."

"You want me to be a zombie."

Oh boy, I thought. He better not say she has the look.

"No," Benny said. "You'd be a beach runner, a real live person. You'd do a couple scenes with the star. Get paid, too."

Stella's squint vanished. "Paid? As in cash?"

"Yeah. It's a good part. Uncle's doing auditions right now, down at the beach."

Stella studied Benny.

Bunched her lips, puffed up her cheeks.

Benny took off his mirror shades and looked into her eyes. "Come meet him."

She turned to stare off into space.

Then looked back at Benny. "So what are we waiting for?"

# 3

## Auditions

So that was how Julio, Maya, Willy, Rubin, Shayla, and I ended up in line at the beach later that afternoon with about a hundred other dreamers hoping to get in a zombie movie.

Benny's uncle had put an ad in the paper,

and even though Benny said we were in, we still had to try out like everyone else.

Stella came after Mom got home. She didn't want to be seen with a bunch of zomb-idiots, which was what she called us.

Mom and Darci would stop by later.

Julio's brothers ended up following us. But they were smart enough to keep their distance. There were only three of them—Marcus, Diego, and Carlos. Cinco was too young to walk to the beach.

Julio glared at them. "Which one should I kill first?"

"None of them," I said. "What's *wrong* with you today?"

"Nothing."

"Well, stop being so mean."

There were all kinds of people trying out—giants, shrimps, happy fat guys, girls skinny as sticks, old dudes with ponytails, musclemen slippery with oil, moms with squirming babies, dads with grins and toothpicks, and guys like us joking around waiting for a chance to show how good we could act.

"Where'd they all come from?" Maya said.

"The moon," Julio said.

It was like a giant beach party.

"All right!" Rubin said, rubbing his hands together. "This is gonna be awesome!"

Julio coughed a laugh. "I don't think they're going to pick you, Rubin. Zombies are skinny, not puffy. Am I right, Calvin?"

I nodded. "Yeah, but this is Hollywood, right? They can make him up like all goo-goo eyes and rotting flesh. He might even get picked first, because even without makeup he looks like a zombie. I mean, he's got those empty black eyes, right? Like nobody's home."

Julio looked at Rubin. "Good point."

Rubin grinned. "Once I get hired I'll see what I can do for you guys . . . but it might be hard."

"Pshh."

I glanced over at Stella. She was with a group of girls waiting to try out for the beach runner part.

Mr. Obi, Benny's uncle, had long gray hair spiked up every whichaway. He looked like he'd just gotten out of bed. He wore a white shirt that hung down over khaki pants rolled up at the bottom. On his feet were rubber slippers, showing that before he became a famous Hollywood millionaire he was once a local guy like us.

"How come they call us extras?" Shayla asked.

"That's the name for all the actors who just walk around in the background," Willy said. And he should know. His family had moved to Kailua from California, where Hollywood is.

"If they take you, you get paid," I added.

Shayla made big eyes. "Wow, Calvin, you really know stuff."

I ducked my head. "Yeah, well . . ."

Maya grabbed my arm. "She's up."

We all turned. Stella was next in line to say some lines for Mr. Obi, another guy, and a girl not much older than her. They sat in canvas folding chairs with clipboards over crossed legs.

Benny stood behind his uncle, watching.

Mr. Obi handed Stella a piece of paper and nodded for her to study it.

Stella took a glance and looked up, ready.

Mr. Obi raised his coffee cup, motioning for her to begin.

I couldn't hear what she said, but I could almost make up the words as she moved. She didn't just stand there like the girls before her had. She paced, and looked down the beach, and moved her arms around and stuff.

Mr. Obi watched her a moment, then put the cup down and raised his hand for her to stop. He turned and huddled up with the other two movie people.

Benny looked over and gave us a thumbs-up.

Mr. Obi stood and reached out to shake Stella's hand. She was the first one he'd done that with.

Our line started moving, everyone bunching up, pushing us ahead. If we put our arms out we'd look like a giant centipede to a bird.

"Here we go," Willy said.

# 4

# A Star is Born

"Listen up, folks," someone called. "We're going to take you off in groups, so pay attention."

I turned away from Stella, who was now swallowed up by movie people.

The girl with a clipboard herded us into a group of kids who were mostly our age. Someone else took the older people to another area.

The girl nodded at us, as if she liked what she saw. "Good morning," she said. "My name is Lana. I'm Mr. Obi's assistant director. It's great to see you all here today."

"Good morning," Shayla said back.

I elbowed her—Don't be such a teacher's pet.

Shayla giggled.

Jeese.

Lana studied us, tapping a pencil against her cheek. Then, like in a dog show, she pointed to the people she wanted.

"You, you, you, you . . . and you six." Me, Willy, Julio, Rubin, Maya, and Shayla. "All of you, move over here."

Dang. Were we out already?

To the other group, Lana said, "The rest of you can go home or stay and watch if you like. This group is all I need.

30

Thank you for coming to try out. We appreci-
ate it. Feel free to have something to eat at the
snack table."

All right! We made it!

"Yahh!" I shouted. Then I realized I was
hugging Shayla. I broke away
fast. "Uhh . . ."

Shayla smiled with dreamy
eyes.

Aiy.

Some kids ran to the food
table. Others slunk away, all
huffy-puffy. But most stayed
to hang out at the beach and
watch. What else was there
to do?

"All right, people,"
Lana said to us. "You are
my zombie kids. Every-
thing you do here over the
next week will be un-
der my direction. Are
you all free next Friday

night, and all day Saturday and maybe Sunday?"

We all nodded.

"So, I'm assuming you've all seen a zombie movie before, right?"

"Yeah-yeah," Rubin said. "Lots."

I said I had, too, but I hadn't. Not even a cartoon one.

But Willy had, and I'd heard Tito talk about one once at school, and sometimes on the playground we staggered around like zombies to be funny.

"So," Lana said. "There are basically two types, slow and fast. The zombies in this film will be the slow type. They're serious and relentless. They have no facial expressions and say nothing. All they want is food, and they'll stop at nothing to get it. Got it?"

Yeah, we all said. Easy. Let's go.

"Great. Okay. So, show me your best zombie walk."

Lana stood back and studied us as we all did our best slow stagger.

Down the beach the older group was doing the same thing. "Look how funny," Julio said, grinning at them. "We must look like idiots to people who don't know what's going on."

True. It was hilarious.

Julio's grin fell off his face when he saw his brothers watching him.

"Forget them," I said. "Don't ruin it."

Julio spat.

I had no idea what a zombie walked like, so I watched everyone else and did that. Stagger. Shuffle. Limp. Make your arms like wet spaghetti. Let your jaw hang open. Don't blink. Look ugly, look dead, look hungry.

Actually, I was hungry, so that part was easy.

Lana waved her hand after a few minutes. "All right, I think we can work with all of you. Come over here and give me your names and phone numbers. And I have a form that your parents need to fill out. We'll start shooting next weekend, right here on this beach. Can you all make it even if you have to get up early?"

*Yeah!* I wanted to shout.

Instead I said, "Sure," with a serious look. After all, we were movie stars now and had to act like it.

Lana grinned. "Good. Practice your moves between now and next weekend, and if you can, watch a zombie movie or two."

I bumped Julio with my elbow. "First we were bored, and now we're going to be in a movie! Can you believe it?"

Julio grunted while Maya jumped up and down holding hands with Shayla, shouting, "We're in a movie, we're in a movie!"

Benny Obi walked over to celebrate with us. "I told you it was for real."

"You were right, Benny," I said. "You didn't make this one up."

"Of course I was right."

"What about Stella?"

"Uncle says every once in a while in the movie business a real artist shows up out of nowhere. Like Stella. She got the part."

"An *artist?*" I frowned. "No way."

Benny raised his eyebrows. "Uncle likes her."

I glanced over at Stella, who was talking with some blond kid. "Is that the star? The guy she's talking to?"

"Yup. Spike Black. Eighteen, and already he's made seven movies. He lives in Beverly Hills, you heard of that place?"

"Of course," I said. *"Beverly Hills Cop."*

"Right. Good movie. Anyway, in the movie Spike is going to save Stella from the zombies."

"Wow," I whispered.

Julio leaned close and waggled his eyebrows. "A star is born."

# 5

## GNOME

"Don't forget to practice," Rubin called as he and Shayla headed home.

Shayla waved. "Bye, Calvin."

"Yeah, yeah," I mumbled.

Man, had I dodged a bullet. It seemed like nobody had seen me hug her. I liked Shayla . . .

but not in public, where my friends could tease me about it.

The rest of us went back to Julio's front yard to practice, parent forms folded up in our pockets and Julio's brothers buzzing around us like bees. I could hardly wait for Mom to get home from shopping.

When her car finally turned down our street, I ran out and raised my hand like a cop stopping traffic.

Mom braked and stuck her head out the window. "Something wrong, Officer?"

"We got in the movie!"

Mom tilted her head. "You did? Congratulations!"

"Thanks. All of us did, and some other friends from school, even Stella—we're actors now . . . like in Hollywood."

"Hollywood?" Darci said, leaning across Mom's lap.

"Yeah, Darce, a for-real Hollywood movie."

"Wow!"

"Well, come on home and tell us all about it," Mom said.

"We're zombies."

Mom laughed and drove away.

"Laters," I said to my friends.

"Show me your stagger," Julio called as I headed home.

I zigzagged back and forth across the street. Julio's brothers ran out to join me. *"Zombie Zumba!"* I shouted, dragging one foot after Mom's car.

Streak, who'd spent the hot afternoon sleeping in the shady garage, trotted out as Mom pulled up.

"Hey, girl," I said, squatting down to greet her. "Too bad dogs can't be zombies. I could get you in the movies."

Mom and Darci got out. There were about a hundred shopping bags on the backseat.

"So, tell me," Mom said.

I told her about Mr. Obi and his movie, and then about how we got parts. I pulled out the parent consent form and unfolded it. "You have to sign this."

Mom took it.

"Stella got a bigger part. But prob'ly only because she's kind of, you know ... pigheaded."

Mom laughed. "Pigheaded?"

I shrugged. "Benny said he was looking for someone with an attitude."

"Hmm. Well, let's go see what Stella can tell us."

Stella was out back sitting in a plastic patio chair, reading something. Darci ran and jumped on her old swing set.

"Stella," Mom said. "Calvin tells me the two of you got parts in a movie. Sounds exciting. Tell me about it."

Stella held up what she'd

been reading. *Zombie Zumba*. She handed Mom the bound stack of paper. "This is the screenplay."

Darci started swinging. The rusty chains squeaked and squealed:

*Give.*

*Us.*

*Oil.*

*Give.*

*Us.*

*Oil.*

Mom read the title. "'Written by Thor Obi.' What an interesting name."

"That's Benny's uncle, Mom." I tapped his name on the script. "He's the director and producer, too."

Mom handed the script back. "Tell me about your part."

Stella shrugged. "It's just a small one, but I have a few lines. There's a form you have to sign first."

"Lines?" I said. "Don't they know that when you open your mouth the camera will break?"

Stella squinted at me. "Tread lightly, little man, or I might get the director to fire you."

"He won't fire me just because you said."

"Sure he will. I'll ask, How can an ignorant gnome be a zombie? It wouldn't be realistic."

"A what?"

"See what I mean? You're ignorant. Don't know anything. He'll fire you in a flash."

Heat swelled on my face, but I decided I'd better quit now, because maybe she *could* get me fired. And anyway, what was a gnome?

Mom stepped in. "You two need to give each other a break. What do you say? Can you do that?"

I mashed my lips. "Yeah. I guess."

Stella nodded.

"Good. Now let's go see what we can scrape up for dinner."

Stella waved the script in my face. "Too bad gnomes can't read, because you might learn what this story is about."

I batted it away.

Stella laughed. "Gnome."

Out in the yard, Darci pumped away on the swing, humming with her eyes closed.

I had to find a dictionary.

# 6

## The Inner Zombie

That night after dinner I was in the kitchen with Mom when her boyfriend, Ledward, came over. He clapped his hand on my shoulder. "I hear you had a big day."

"I'm going to be in a movie! At the beach."

Ledward looked down at me. He was about ten feet tall, a huge Hawaiian-Filipino guy.

"I heard somebody talking about that when I was standing in line at Foodland."

"Yeah, and me and my friends are in it."

"Well, congratulations. That's a big deal. You call your dad yet?"

I shook my head.

"Call him. He'll want to know about it."

My dad was a singer, Little Johnny Coconut. He lived in Las Vegas now, and he had a new wife, Marissa. I wasn't sure if I should tell him about the movie, because he was already a star and being a zombie probably wasn't a big thing to him. "Sure," I said.

Ledward ruffled my hair. "Good."

He was fresh out of the shower and had come over to take Mom and Darci out for a ride. Mom told me he'd spent the day cleaning out Blackie's mud pit. Blackie was his pet pig that used to be a wild one but liked people now. Sometimes Ledward drove him around in his jeep.

When Darci came into the kitchen and saw Ledward she jumped up. Ledward grabbed

her around her waist and lifted her over his head.

"You ready for some ice cream, Darci girl?"

Darci shrieked as Ledward swooped her back down to the floor. "Double scoops?" she said.

"Triple."

Darci turned to Mom. "Mom, get ready! Let's go!"

Ledward lifted his chin toward me. "How about you, boy? You want to come along?"

"Can't. Gotta rehearse. Stella's going to be in it, too, and so are my friends, and we're getting *paid*."

"Paid!" he said. "Sounds like serious business."

"That's why I have to stay and practice."

46

Ledward nodded. "What's your part?"

"Zombie."

Ledward chuckled. "That would be the part I would want, too. What's Stella?"

"Beach runner. She gets to talk, but we just groan."

"She must have some talent."

I made a face. "I guess."

Ledward patted my shoulder. "Maybe we can bring something back for you."

Mom, Darci, and Ledward left, and I got ready to practice my part.

Only I had no idea what to do.

I crept down the hall to Stella's room.

"Stella," I said through her closed door. "I . . . I need to see that script."

"Beat it."

"No, I gotta see what my part is."

She swung open the door and stood looking at me with her hands on her hips. "You're a zombie. What else is there to know? They don't speak, so there's nothing for you to read in the script. You just walk around in a daze like you always do. Simple."

"That's all?"

"What do you think, Stump? Do you even know what a zombie is? Have you ever even seen a zombie movie?"

I frowned. "No."

She hesitated. "Never?"

"Never."

"Oh my gosh, this is too funny. An ignorant gnome zombie who doesn't even know what he is."

"I know what a gnome is. I looked it up."

"Look." She grabbed my arm and pulled me into her room. "Watch me. This is how zombies walk."

She let go and stood frozen with her eyes closed.

"What are you doing?" I said.

"Shhh. I'm calling up my inner zombie. If you can do that you can *become* that zombie, understand? You have to imagine the part first. You have to visualize."

"What's that mean?"

"See it in your head. That's what actors do. They become their characters and then they act. Now be quiet."

I waited for almost a full minute.

Stella didn't move a muscle. It was like she died standing up.

Creepy.

When her eyes popped open I let out a gasp. Stella wasn't Stella anymore.

Her eyes went blank. Her arms fell limp. Her mouth sagged like at the dentist. She looked like a toad squashed on the road, and when she staggered toward me with her hands out like claws, I banged down the hall and ran out the screen door into the front yard.

Man, she could act!

*That* was what zombies were supposed to look like?

Inside the house Stella was laughing her head off.

It was dark by then. Lights were on in the houses on our street. But nobody was out. I was alone.

I cringed.

"Okay," I said to myself. "You can do this."

I stood still and closed my eyes, like Stella had. "Come on up," I said to the zombie inside me.

I waited.

Nothing.

Not even a zombie burp.

I peeked one eye open to see if my inner zombie was standing next to me or something.

The street was still empty, except for Maya's cat, Zippy, who'd shown up to hunt mice.

I closed my eyes again. "Inner zombie," I said. "Come on up!"

I swayed to the side and lost my balance. I opened my eyes just before I knocked over our mailbox.

My inner zombie was waking up.

"Ahh!" I shrieked, and Zippy took off like a bullet.

Maybe I just got dizzy.

# 7

# Blue Lights Spinning

The next day, Sunday, I woke up in a sweat.

I'd been dreaming of zombies. One long nightmare, because they all looked like Stella!

I stumbled out of my room, which was made out of half the garage. I nearly banged into the lawn mower.

Streak, who'd slept on the bunk below me, headed out to the yard.

I went into the kitchen.

Darci was eating a bowl of cereal at the counter.

"Who's up?" I asked.

"Just me."

I nodded and got myself a glass of guava juice and a bowl of Grape Nuts with honey.

Stella's script was over by the phone. I grabbed it and took it to the counter and sat next to Darci.

"What's that?" she asked.

"This," I said, tapping it with my finger, "is a movie script."

Darci shrugged.

I started reading.

And reading.

By the time I'd finished the whole thing, Darci was long gone and Mom had come into the kitchen.

"Mom, this movie is really good!"

"Is that Stella's script?"

"Yeah, and in it the zombies come marching up onto the beach from underwater. They went down with a ship coming to Hawaii from the Philippines, and they just started walking on the bottom of the ocean, and then they come walking up on Kailua beach. It's so cool!"

"Well, then you better have a good breakfast."

"We're not filming until next week. But anyway, in the movie there's this young scientist who saves everyone from the zombies because he's a genius and invents a way to trap them and destroy them."

Mom smiled. "Sounds lovely, Cal."

"I gotta practice. Last night Stella showed me how to call up my inner zombie to get ready for the part."

Mom laughed. "Inner zombie?"

"Yeah!" I ran outside, Streak trotting along with me down to Julio's house.

I went around back and peeked through the screen on his bedroom window. I could see him sleeping. "Julio! Wake up! We need to practice."

He rolled over and popped up on one elbow. He squinted my way. "What time is it?"

"Zombie time. Get up."

He flopped back down. "Zombies need their sleep."

"No! They don't sleep. I read it in the script. They're always awake."

He popped back up. "You read the script?"

"Yeah. Stella left it out."

"Be right there."

A half hour later Julio and I were out on the street with Willy and Maya.

Maya yawned and rubbed her face. "This better be good, Calvin. Do you know what time it is?"

"Yeah, time to practice."

"It's eleven-twenty, way too early for this."

"Real actors don't worry what time it is, so listen. Stella showed me how actors get ready for their parts. First you have to become your character by calling it up."

Julio shoved Willy toward his house. "Go get your mom's phone."

"Shhh," I said. "Let me finish. You got to close your eyes and call up your inner zombie, and not on a phone, you goofball. Here. Do it like this."

I showed them what Stella did . . . only my inner zombie was still asleep, so I faked it.

"You got us up for *this*?" Maya said.

"It works. Stella said."

So we all stood there with our eyes closed at the edge of the road in front of Maya's house.

"Yah!" Maya yelped.

I opened my eyes. "What?"

"I saw it! I saw the zombie inside me."

Julio took a step away from Maya.

Willy gaped at her. "You *saw* it?"

Maya put a finger to her lips and closed her eyes again.

We waited, glancing at each other.

"Weird," Julio mouthed, and spun his finger around his ear.

*"Yaaahh!"* Maya yelped again.

Her eyes popped open. Her face went flat. She started staggering toward us.

We backed away.

"Come on, fools," she said, cracking up. "Get with it."

"Jeese, Maya," Julio said. "You didn't have to scare us."

She lurched toward him. "I'm hungry for your brains."

"Zombies don't talk," he said.

"This one does."

All right! We were practicing. We were actors on our way to becoming Hollywood millionaires like Benny's uncle.

We spent the next hour staggering around in the middle of the road. It was fun.

Until a car turned down our street.

Blue lights spinning.

# 8

# Zombie cops

The police car pulled up to us and stopped.

A cop got out. A *big* cop. Ten feet tall . . . maybe eleven.

Four zombies gaped up at him.

"What's going on, boys?" He nodded to Maya. "And girl."

I gulped. "Uh, we were just . . . um, practicing."

He glanced down the street and I turned to see what he was looking at. Mrs. Costello, who lived next to Julio, was peeking out her front window.

The officer turned back. "Practicing what?"

"Being zombies," Maya said. "We're going to be in a movie."

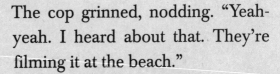

The cop grinned, nodding. "Yeah-yeah. I heard about that. They're filming it at the beach."

The spinning blue lights were like magnets to Julio's four brothers, who were now out in their front yard staring at us.

Julio squinted at them. Still looking at his brothers, he said to the cop, "We got parts, and we're getting paid a hundred dollars . . . each!"

"Good pay."

"Did we do something wrong, Officer?" I asked.

"Not that I can see," he said. "We got a call. I came to check it out."

"A call?" Willy asked. "Why?"

"Well, a lady said there were a bunch of kids stumbling around in the middle of the street, and she was worried that maybe something was wrong with them . . . like maybe they were drunk or something."

I gaped at him. "Drunk?"

"Well, I can see that you're not, of course. But why don't you show me what you were doing."

We limped and shuffled and staggered for him, giving it all we had. I thought we looked pretty good. We were getting it down.

The officer rubbed his chin. "You folks ever seen a zombie movie?"

"Only Willy," I said.

The cop nodded. "Watch. This is how they walk."

He did a walk that was like a corpse dragging his foot.

I liked it and grinned at Julio.

"See?" the cop said. "I'm hungry, just looking for food. That's all I want. Food in the form of your brains. That's what zombies like best."

"Walking dead," Willy said.

"You got it. The walking dead."

All of us started dragging our feet in the middle of the street, doing what the cop was doing. So crazy!

Now Mrs. Costello was out in her yard, scowling, hands on her hips.

A minute later, another police car came cruising down the street. It pulled up behind the first one. Two cars with blue lights flashing.

The officer got out, a short Japanese guy with muscles so big they were about to rip his shirt.

The first cop said, "Hey, Jacob. These kids are in that movie they're shooting at the beach next weekend. Supposed to be zombies, but they don't know the walk. I'm showing them."

The second cop's face turned from serious to mischievous. "Well, I saw *Shaun of the Dead.* Was good. They walked like this."

Now there were six of us lurching around in the street.

And Mrs. Costello was about to explode. Her face was as pinched and puckered as chewed-up bubble gum.

"Uh, Jacob," the first cop said. "We have a concerned citizen watching us."

Both officers stood up straighter and got that serious police look back.

Then the second cop waved his hand

around like he was mad at us. But he said the opposite. "Stop laughing. I'm chewing you out. Play along before she calls the chief. It's really going to be fun for you to be in that movie, and you're getting the look down pretty good. But go find someplace else to practice, because you're freaking out that poor lady."

He almost grinned, then scowled.

"Go!" he said, loud enough for Mrs. Costello to hear.

The other cop whispered, "We'll go talk to her. I bet she doesn't know what a zombie is."

"Tell her we ate too much kimchee and got sick," I said.

The tall cop laughed. "I actually did that once."

The cops walked down to see Mrs. Costello.

"Zombie cops," Maya said. "Crazy."

Julio's brothers were mimicking us in their yard. Julio's face turned red. "I'm going to put sand between their sheets."

I pulled him away. "Come."

We went out onto the golf course that ran behind Maya's and Willy's houses and practiced until some golfers came and yelled at us.

What was wrong with people? Didn't they like to have fun anymore?

"You think Benny's uncle is really a millionaire?" Julio asked.

"Sure," I said. "Benny said so."

Maya laughed. "Come on, Calvin. Half of what he tells us is made up."

"True."

"I believe it," Willy said.

"What's not true is that he wrote that movie with his uncle," Julio spat. "I don't believe that for a second."

I frowned. I'd thought that, too.

Willy shrugged. "Who cares? Benny's fun. I like him."

I nodded. "Me too."

"He just makes things up to make himself look good," Julio said. "He's such a liar."

"He's not a liar," I said.

Julio scoffed.

"How come you're in such a bad mood?"

"I'm not. I'm just being real."

I shook my head. The truth was, I didn't know what to think about Benny. Or Julio, being so mean.

"Hey," I said to change the subject. "How about we zombie over to my house and scare up something to eat?"

Maya grinned. "Brains."

"Oops," Julio said. "There's a problem. No brains at Calvin's house."

"You punk." I shoved him, and everyone cracked up.

Bad mood or not, I had the best friend ever.

# 9

# Red-Eyed Silver Skull

At school that week we spent every recess zombie walking. We had the whole school doing it, too . . . until Mrs. Leonard, the principal, told us to stop fooling around.

"This is an educational institution," she said. "Not an insane asylum."

For real, nobody liked to have fun anymore.

Except in class.

"My little zombies," our teacher, Mr. Purdy, said on Friday before school got out. "Who's going to be in the movie this weekend?"

Six hands shot up.

"I am, Mr. Purdy," Rubin said, waving for attention.

Ace, behind me, shouted, "Me too. I got hired for pay."

Mr. Purdy nodded. "Pay is good."

I turned to Ace. "I didn't see you at the tryouts. Where were you?"

"I came late. But got in anyway. They liked that I'm handsome." He grinned.

"But zombies are ugly."

"Contrast. Make you look uglier than you are."

"Look!" Rubin said, making a lifeless face. "I like eat brains."

Maya snorted. "Too bad you already ate yours."

The class burst out laughing.

"Mr. Purdy," I said. "You remember Benny Obi? The director is his uncle."

"Well, I'll be danged."

"I know kung fu," Julio called, and everyone laughed harder.

Mr. Purdy shuffled. He raised his claws and drooped his face. "Feed me," he slurred in a deep voice. "Brains or guts, gimme soy sauce and I don't care."

He was all right, Mr. Purdy.

After dinner that night we all went down to the beach, including Ledward, who wanted to bring Blackie along. But he figured a pet pig might not be welcome on a movie set.

I met up with Julio, Maya, Willy, Rubin, Shayla, and Benny.

"Too bad pigs can't be zombies," I said to Benny. "That would be unique."

"Unique is zombies coming out of the ocean," he said. "Nobody did that before."

I nodded.

"My uncle's a genius. That's why he's a millionaire. I'm going to be a millionaire, too."

I laughed. "Prob'ly."

The extras gathered around Mr. Obi.

Mom, Ledward, and Darci stood around the edges with Julio's, Willy's, and Maya's parents and a couple hundred other people trying to see.

Julio's brothers crept close with monkey eyes. Julio shook his fist at them and they stuck out their tongues.

Mr. Obi stood on a wooden box and raised his hands for everyone to be quiet.

"Thank you all for coming. We've filmed a lot of this story already at a studio in California. But the beach scenes we will be filming this weekend are absolutely critical."

Everyone clapped and cheered.

Mr. Obi went on. "I need all of you here at three-thirty tomorrow morning."

A low gasp rattled through the crowd.

"In the *morning*?" Maya said.

Benny grinned. "Yup."

Mr. Obi held up his hands. "That's early, but it's important. The sun rises around six-thirty, and we have to get everyone made up and ready to shoot by five-forty-five. We'll start just before the sun comes up, when the sky is still black, but way out to sea a faint glow will start to spread across the horizon."

Benny leaned close. "The most peaceful time of day," he said, low. "Or the spookiest."

Yai!

Mr. Obi spoke a while longer, then waved. "See you all tomorrow, bright and early."

Benny made a small frame with his thumb and fingers and pointed it at the ocean. "Picture it—the dead coming out of the sea."

I imagined walking corpses rising out of the ocean while everyone was still sleeping. No one would even suspect it.

Man, that would be major-major chicken skin.

But right now it was major-major fun. Not only were hundreds of people at the beach, there were also big trucks and tables and lanterns and families sitting around on blankets, and someone was playing Hawaiian slack key guitar.

Julio's parents came up to us. "Julio," his mom said, "would you please watch your brothers while your dad and I take a walk on the beach?"

That was it for Julio. "Why do I have to do everything? What's wrong with them looking after themselves? What am I, a slave?"

Whoa!

Julio's mom looked at him with her mouth open.

"I mean it!" Julio stormed away.

Julio's dad watched Julio walk off. "You go on with the boys. I'll catch up later."

He headed down the beach after Julio.

The brothers leaped like fleas around Julio's mom. "Let's go, let's go!"

Julio's mom took them down to the sand.

Me and my friends stood in silence.

Finally, Willy said, "Wow. Julio cracked."

We all went down to the edge of the ocean to stand with our feet in the water.

"So tell us about tomorrow, Benny," I said, trying to lighten things up. "We come out of the ocean and then what?"

"Try to see it in your head. First we go all the way under the water, and then when Un-

cle gives the signal, we come up, slow, slow, slow and creep toward shore."

Willy scrunched up his face. "But won't the makeup and stuff wash off?"

"Waterproof. Plus, we have rubber masks, and eyeballs that pop out. Everything will be fine. You'll see. We know what we're doing."

"That's right, Willy," I said. "Benny knows what he's doing."

"How do you know?"

"Look what's around his neck."

Willy and Rubin bent close to look at the silver skull with red eyes hanging on a chain.

Willy frowned. "What am I supposed to see?"

"That skull used to be his cousin's head." I grinned, making it up. "He got infected and became a zombie, and when he died, they shrunk it and dipped it in silver. Whenever he has a problem, Benny talks to it. And that's why he knows stuff."

Benny laughed. "That's good, Calvin. I'm going to remember that one."

Willy looked at Rubin. "Ready?"

Rubin grinned.

"Hey!" I yelped as they picked me up and threw me in the ocean.

I came up laughing.

# 10

## Wild Hair and Drooping Eyeballs

Getting up at three o'clock the next morning was no party. I set my alarm and put it on the windowsill right by my top bunk. When it went off I didn't know where I was.

I rubbed my eyes and leaned over the edge to see if Streak's dark shape was there.

"Zombie day," I mumbled, rolling back on my bed.

Zombie day!

Instantly, my mind was as sharp as a machete. I climbed down and got dressed, then crept into the house. Lazybones Streak didn't even peek open an eye. But she couldn't come with me anyway.

It was dark. No one was up.

Mom had said she would come to the beach with Darci and Stella around eight. Stella wasn't doing her part until later.

I grabbed a bowl and a box of cereal.

Fifteen minutes later I was heading down to the beach with Julio, Willy, and Maya.

Julio seemed extra quiet, like he still had stuff on his mind. So I kept my mouth shut. I'd ask him later if he got chewed out by his dad.

We walked in silence. That's how it is when you get up early. You just think and look at stuff until you're ready to wake up.

The huge crowd of the night before was now a small army of people running around under the bright glare of portable lights. A mass of black power cords snaked out from one of the big trucks idling in the beach parking

lot. It hummed loudly, probably waking up everyone in the houses nearby. Benny said it was a generator truck that made electricity for the equipment.

I spotted Rubin and Shayla at a long table with some other soon-to-be dead people, including Ace from school. We headed over to them, staying clear of the guys moving lights and other equipment around.

"Hey!" Rubin pointed with his chin. "Here come the costumes."

Guys rolled two racks of raggedy-looking rags over to the table.

Shayla giggled. "Ooo, I love this!"

Within minutes we were wearing those rags, and right after that people were painting our faces and going over our costumes with pins in their mouths. When I looked in a mirror I couldn't believe it was me. My eyes looked bruised, and my face was like I was sick. Someone pulled a rubber wig with scraggly hair over my head.

Holy baloney! I was a corpse!

"You lucky," I said to Rubin, who got a mask with a hanging eyeball. "I want one like that."

Willy looked Rubin over. "Can you see?"

"Sure. My good eye still works."

Maya and Shayla got torn, dirty dresses, and wigs with wild hair that went every whichaway. "This fake hair will still stick up even in the water," Maya said. "Touch it."

It felt rubbery. "Cool."

Willy and Julio got ripped shirts and shorts. Their legs were painted with streaks of gray and purple-black.

Benny walked up with an arm that showed the bone coming out. "Ho!" I said, stepping back. "That looks real!"

"You like it? I made it myself."

"Really?"

"Uncle's teaching me everything from makeup to set design to editing. I made some of the sets in *My Cousin Is a Teenage Vambie,* too."

"You did?"

"Yeah. At the studio in Hollywood."

"Wow, you are so lucky."

"Not luck. Talent."

Benny looked away. Like even he didn't believe what he was saying.

"Can you show us how to have talent, too?"

"Yeah," Julio said. "We need some talent."

Willy squeezed in. "Show us."

Benny brightened, like a light switched back on. "Just watch what I do and do that."

We stood around with the rest of the zombies. Thirty-eight of us, young and old. I knew Ace was there, but I sure couldn't tell which one he was.

Before we started Mr. Obi checked everyone over. "You're better zombies than the ones in my last film. This is going to be great. Okay, here's the story."

Mr. Obi rubbed his hands together, his eyes twinkling like polished dimes. "You zombies invaded a ship that sailed out of Manila and killed everyone aboard. Then the ship sank in a storm. You are the only survivors. Except technically, since you're dead, you didn't survive."

Everyone mumbled a laugh.

"You ended up sinking to the bottom of the sea."

"We didn't drown?" somebody asked.

"Nope. Zombies are already dead, so when you hit bottom you just started walking. It took you weeks, but here you are about to come out onto land again. We will film you coming from the sea in the early-morning light."

My cheeks hurt from smiling. This was so cool!

Mr. Obi clapped his hands. "Ready?"

"Yeah!"

Me, Willy, and Julio were grinning like donkeys and banging each other with our shoulders. Julio was coming back to his old self now, and that felt really good.

"Remember," Mr. Obi went on. "You rise up out of the ocean slowly, then shuffle toward shore, where you limp around dazed and confused, and don't forget you're hungry—really, really hungry. I want to see starvation all over your faces."

"Do we eat?" I whispered to Benny.

"No, you just look around and wander along the beach. We'll film what happens next later today, and some more tonight."

Mr. Obi checked the cameras, lights, and reflectors that were set up along the top of the beach. One guy marked numbers on a slate, and three other guys set up long poles with microphones on the end.

Lana, the assistant director, ran around telling people what to do, watching over everything all at once.

Dawn hadn't broken yet. The dim lights made it look like there was a moon out. My friends' dead-looking faces gave me the shivers.

"All right," Mr. Obi called. "Into the water. On my signal, submerge yourselves entirely, count to five, then slowly come up and slog toward shore."

We headed toward the black ocean with the sun's faint glow just beginning to appear on the horizon.

The water was warm. Except for the sound of small, never-ending waves slapping the sand, the whole world was silent.

I waded out up to my neck and waited for the signal.

Being in the ocean at night was awesome . . . until I thought about sharks.

Don't think about that now!

Onshore, unseen behind the eerie glow of movie lights, Mr. Obi called, "Get ready."

I took a deep breath.

"Action!"

I sank down into a world of snapping and clicking sea creatures, bazillions of them, large and small.

A whole other world.

I started counting.

One.

Two.

Three . . .

# 11

## Zombies on the Beach

Creeping up out of the ocean with silent zombies all around me was the spookiest, bone-chillingest experience I ever had in my whole entire life!

Just ahead of me, Maya's wild wig was wet and dripping, and her arms, painted brown and green with fake bones, hung at her sides like on a half-rotted, meaty skeleton.

The sun glowed brighter behind the horizon. Colors started to come alive on the beach, shadows turning into things I could recognize.

I crept closer. Up to my waist, my knees.

Slow, slow, slow.

We made shore, looking lost, hungry.

The warm ocean rolled off me, dripping to the sand.

Behind the eerie movie lights I could see silent people watching us.

I started limping and dragging one foot. It was so fun I had to work hard to keep from smiling at Julio.

We wandered around the beach for about five minutes before Mr. Obi called, "Cut!"

"That means stop," Benny said.

The sky was purple and pink, with blue on the way as the sun peeked up over the horizon. Mr. Obi raised his hands as if to say, Yeah! You did it!

I grinned at my friends.

The camera crew began hauling their equipment down onto the sand. Mr. Obi pointed here and there, tossing orders around.

"All right!" he called to us. "We're going to shoot more of you on the beach. Just wander around aimlessly, and don't go up to the houses. We'll do that later. Sort of stay in the same area and look hungry."

"I really *am* hungry," I muttered to Julio.

"Yeah, me too. Maybe they'll give us breakfast."

"Shhh." Benny nodded toward his uncle. "Listen for the cue."

Mr. Obi spoke through a megaphone. "Mill around until you hear music. When you hear that, turn and start walking toward it. Slowly, remember. You've been walking underwater for weeks. You're tired, weakened, waterlogged dead people."

That made me laugh.

"Ready! Action!"

We limped around looking confused and hungry, which was easy. The hard part was to keep from laughing every time I passed my friends, especially Rubin, who was probably the best zombie of us all. He had it down good.

Were Mom and Darci here yet? Were they watching?

I was jolted out of my daydreaming when somebody's dog came running down from a house.

Benny started limping toward it.

The dog backed away. It didn't know what to make of that ugly thing coming at him.

Benny kept going.

Finally the dog took off and Benny lurched back.

The sun, now climbing into the sky, flooded the beach with new light.

We were almost to the cameras before Mr. Obi called, "Cut!"

I stopped in my tracks and stood frozen.

"S'all right," Benny said. "The scene is over. You don't have to freeze."

"Oh."

"When do we eat?" Rubin asked.

"Soon," Benny said. "Brains on toast."

# 12

## Cow Brains

Standing in line with a bunch of zombies waiting to eat wasn't something we did every day. It was past nine o'clock, and Mom, Ledward, Darci, and Stella had showed up. When Mom saw us she thought we looked so funny she ran home to get her camera. Actually, she said we looked *precious*.

Hunh?

The line was slow, but the food smelled good—pancakes, bacon, scrambled eggs, and hot chocolate.

"Hey, Benny," Julio said. "Remember the time you ate bugs at school? That was so gross. I don't even know how you did that."

"Pfft," Benny said. "That was nothing. One time I ate real brains."

He gave us a blank look, waiting for what he knew would come next.

We said it together. "What!"

Benny shrugged. "In *My Cousin Is a Teenage Vambie,* my uncle wanted us to act like we were really eating brains. So we did, just to see what it was like. Cow brains."

Maya covered her ears. "I don't want to hear this."

"They were soft," Benny went on. "They had to be cooked by a specialist, because if you don't cook brains right you could get mad cow disease."

Shayla grimaced. "Eeew."

Benny looked at her. "It didn't taste that bad, really. People eat brains all over the world. Calf brains, mostly. People eat everything. Dogs, cats, insects, skunks–"

"Not," Willy said. "People don't eat skunks."

"Sure they do. They aren't poisonous. You just have to remove the stink gland without breaking it. If you break it you can't eat it."

"That's sick," Willy said.

Benny shrugged.

I glanced toward the food table. Was Mr. Obi going to put brains in the food so we could act better?

Benny elbowed Rubin. "You ever had inago? That's Japanese food."

Rubin grinned. "Fried grasshoppers."

"You can eat them alive, too," Benny went on.

"Crunch," Rubin said.

"*Stop!*" Maya said. "You're ruining my appetite."

"My great-grampa ate them during World War Two," Benny continued. "Just went out and caught them in the grass and ate them. Because food was scarce."

Maya stepped between Benny and Rubin. "If you two don't stop talking about this I'm going to barf, and when I barf I'm going to aim it at you. Got it?"

I pulled Julio aside and whispered, "You think they put brains in that food? If they did it for one zombie movie, they could do it for this one."

Julio frowned. "With Benny anything is possible. Maybe his uncle is *worse* than him. Ever thought of that?"

"Aiy."

Julio dug in his pocket and came up empty. "You got any money?"

"Zero."

"Dang. I was thinking we could get something to eat at Kalapawai Market instead of here."

"Good idea."

Willy poked his head in. "What are you guys whispering about?"

"Benny put brains in the food."

"What food?"

I lifted my chin toward the table of sweet-smelling pancakes and bacon. What a shame to ruin all that good food.

Julio raised his eyebrows. "You never know with Benny, right?"

Willy looked at Benny, who was talking to Rubin about Japan. "What are we gonna do?"

"Come," I said.

"Hey, where you going?" Rubin asked as we left the line. The people behind us moved up and took our spot.

"Not hungry yet," Julio said.

"Yeah, us too," me and Willy said.

Maya was already at the table shoveling

pancakes onto her plate with a white plastic fork.

"Suit yourself," Rubin said.

"We will."

We ran over to Ledward and Mom.

"Stand together," she said, aiming her camera at us.

She took her time focusing. She had to ask Darci where to press. Kids always know stuff their parents don't. Fact of life.

"Can we have some money, Mom?"

*Click.*

"That was a good one. Let's do one more. What do you need money for, sweetie? Do you have to pay for that food? That doesn't seem right."

*Click.*

"No, Mom. It's free. We just want to get something at Kalapawai instead."

Ledward glanced over at the breakfast table. "Looks like a lot of good food is already here."

"Yeah, but . . . come on, Mom. We're hungry. We'd rather have . . . fruit, like papayas and pineapples."

"Here," Ledward said. He dug a ten-dollar bill out of his pocket and handed it to me.

"Thanks!"

But he wouldn't let go of it. He kept his eyes on me. "First, tell my why you don't want to eat that perfectly good food over there."

I looked at Willy and Julio.

They waited with a look that said, Yeah, why?

I yanked the ten dollars out of Ledward's hand. "Just in case they put cow brains in the pancakes."

Ledward's mouth fell open. Then he threw his head back and cracked up.

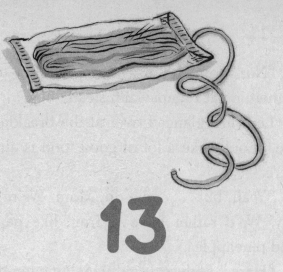

# 13

# Red Licorice

There was a car parked in front of Kalapawai Market. Four guys were standing around it.

"Uh-oh," Julio said.

When we slid to a stop they all turned to look.

One guy in a red shirt laughed. "Look at these dudes."

They all cracked up.

"Hey!" the red shirt guy called to us. "It's Halloween or what?" The other three staggered with laughter.

We slipped past them into the store.

"Get something quick and get out of here," I said. "We look like idiots."

Julio and Willy didn't argue with that.

We grabbed three cone sushis and a big bag of red licorice and hurried back to the beach.

On the way, I said, "So, Julio . . . did your dad chew you out for talking back to your mom last night?"

Julio shrugged. "Not really."

"That's good," I said.

Julio was silent for a moment. Then he stopped and turned to us. He wanted to say something.

"What?" I said.

Julio looked away, then back. "Well . . . my dad . . . he could have grounded me for a month for what I did. And he could have chewed me out, too. But you know what he said?"

"You were grounded for a year?"

"He said we were like the movie."

I cocked my head. "I don't get it."

"Our family is just like Benny's movie. He said everyone in it has a part to play. Some parts are small ones, like us being extras. And some parts are big ones, star parts, like Stella's. And all the parts work together to make the whole thing work."

I nodded. "Yeah, cool."

Julio shook his head. "Then he said . . . in our family my part was a star part, and he was proud of me . . . because without what I do the family wouldn't work so good."

"Wow," Willy said. "And he didn't get mad at you for mouthing off?"

Julio shook his head. "He just said that and walked with me for a while. We talked about fishing."

We fell silent after that, and I thought of how lucky Julio was to have a dad like that.

But I had Ledward . . . and Mom.
And even Dad, sometimes.
We had our movie, too.

 I shook my head. Julio's dad was a smart guy.

We found Rubin,
Benny, Maya, and Shayla
sitting in the shade of the
ironwood trees.

"How come you eating that junks and not pancakes?" Rubin asked.

I grinned. "How did those pancakes taste?"

"Good. I had seconds."

"Then you must be smarter now."

"Hunh?"

"Because those pancakes had cow brains in them."

Rubin stared at me. "What you talking?"

"Tell him, Benny. Your uncle put brains in

it so we could act better, right? Like you did in *My Cousin Is a Teenage Vambie*."

Benny shook his head. "Nope. But so what if he did? Brains got nutrients in it, like vitamins and minerals. If you grow up eating brains you'll have healthier brains than if you didn't. Did you know that?"

"Give me a break," Julio scoffed.

"No, it's true. I read about it in *Scientific American*. Anyway, there wasn't any brains. That food was catered by Zippy's. Was good, too."

"Zippy's!" Willy said, shoving me from behind. "And we missed that for red licorice?"

"Well, I could have been right."

Maya gave me a You-are-so-pathetic look. Shayla gave me a nicer one.

"So," I said. "Anyone want some red licorice?"

We sat around gnawing while the film crew got ready for another scene.

Shayla nudged Benny. "What's next?"

He pointed his chin toward Stella, Mr. Obi, and Spike Black, the star. They were looking at the script. "Zombie Zumba," Benny said, waggling his eyebrows.

I only half heard him as I watched the food crew take away all those sweet-smelling left-overs.

Dang.

# 14

# Steel Cages

Spike Black looked just like he was supposed to—like a movie star. I'd seen him in *Kick Start*, a movie about a super-talented twelve-year-old kid who joined a scrappy high school soccer team and took them all the way to the top. It was pretty good.

He was older now, eighteen.

But even though he was famous he seemed kind of shy. At least, he wasn't running around ordering people to do things for him. He just stood with Stella listening to Mr. Obi.

The other zombies sat around in the sun waiting for something to do. Shayla and Maya had gone down to the beach to cool their feet in the ocean.

"Weird, how they make movies," Julio said. "Not like you see it, but all broken up into pieces. This scene, that scene. It's crazy."

"They put it all together in editing," Benny said. "Like a puzzle. It's fun."

"You've done that?" Willy asked.

"Sure. My uncle is teaching me."

Julio coughed up a laugh. "Like somebody taught you kung fu?"

"Hey," I said. "Look."

A big flatbed truck was growling toward the parking lot. It could hardly squeeze down the road, which was crammed with parked cars.

On the bed of the truck were three huge steel cages, the kind that hold wild animals at the zoo.

"Holy bazooks," I said. "What are *those* for?"

Benny grinned. "You read the script, right? Remember the cages?"

"You mean–"

"Yup. The moonlight scene. Before this day is done we will be captured in those cages, taken out to sea . . . and dumped overboard."

I looked at Julio and Willy. "How cool is that!"

# 15

# Dog Star

"Zombies," Mr. Obi called, motioning for us to gather around him. "Come!"

Somebody had showed up with a dog, but not a dog like Streak, who was a poi dog, a mix. This one was too handsome to be a mutt. A lady stood with him. The dog did whatever she said.

Somebody else showed up, too . . . Julio's brothers.

But this time their dad was with them.

"Look who came," I said to Julio.

Julio watched them. They didn't see us.

"Looks like Pop took a day off," Julio said.

I spotted Mom, Darci, and Ledward in the crowd, watching the dog do tricks.

"That's one nice dog," Willy said.

"Golden retriever," Benny said. "Came over from Los Angeles yesterday. His name is

Alex, and that lady with him is his trainer, Lauren. Best in the business. She once trained a deer to play dead."

"Not," Willy said. "How can you train a deer?"

Benny shrugged. "She can."

"Holy guacamole!"

I gasped as she made the dog jump up as high as her shoulder.

We bunched up around Mr. Obi.

"Okay, everyone," he said. "Here's how it's going down. Lauren, bring Alex over."

I felt somebody snuggle up next to me.

A zombie . . . named Shayla.

She smiled and whispered, "You having a good time, Calvin?"

"Uh . . . yeah, but shhh. He's talking now."

Shayla pinched her finger and thumb together and zipped her lips.

"All right, listen up, folks," Mr. Obi said. "First get checked out by makeup. Then go back down on the beach. We're shooting two scenes in one this time. You're more like background, at least for a few minutes."

Hey! We were part of Stella's scene. How could she call me ignorant if we were both in the same scene? She must be a gnome, too.

That made me smile.

Alex, the retriever, lounged on the grass with his tongue drooping in the heat. Looked

half asleep. I whispered to Benny, "What if that dog doesn't want to act?"

"Don't worry. Lauren can make it sing if she wants. She can make it eat popcorn, then pick its teeth with a toothpick."

"Pshh," I scoffed.

That dog looked bored. It might take a firecracker to get that lazybones up and going.

As we headed over to the makeup table I spotted Stella. She was dressed to look like a beach runner, with black shorts and a sky-blue tank top. Her hair hung like a tail from the back of a yellow ball cap.

She saw me watching her and waved.

I lifted my chin.

Making movies makes you be nicer to people, I guess, because Stella even smiled at me.

Mr. Obi rubbed his hands together. "Here we go! Let's try to get this in one take."

All us zombies headed back down to where we'd first come out of the water.

"Action!"

I grinned at Julio and started limping around again.

Shayla shuffled up and followed me. Dang. When the movie comes out everyone is going to see us together, me and my zombie girl-friend.

But then I thought, Nah. Nobody will even recognize us, since we're dead.

A few minutes later Alex the dog came barking down the beach as if he'd read the script and was saying his lines. Amazing.

Could I train Streak to act? I already trained her to chase bufos and sleep on my bottom bunk.

Slowly, we turned toward the barking dog.

In the trees above the beach I could see cameras on Stella, who was trying to run after the dog. But Spike had his arms around her, pulling her back.

"Cut!" Mr. Obi called through a bullhorn. "Let's try that again, and no one look up at the camera, okay?"

This time, we got it right.

Back up in the beach park I found Mom, Darci, and Ledward in the crowd. They'd watched Stella play her part and were congratulating her.

"Did you see me, too, Mom?" I asked.

"Sure did. You make a handsome zombie, sweetie."

I frowned. "Zombies are ugly, Mom, not handsome."

She pinched my cheek. "You will never be ugly to me."

When Julio's brothers came sprinting toward us, Julio said, "I'm outta here!"

"Wait!" I said, grabbing his arm. "Look

at them. They're not coming to bother you; they're coming to see you up close, because to them, you're a movie star."

Julio decided to wait when he saw his dad following.

"Remember what your dad said about your part?"

The brothers stopped a few feet away and stared at us, eyes popping.

Julio stood taller, nodding slowly.

"What a job, Julio!" his dad said. "You boys are natural-born zombies."

Julio grinned and looked at his feet.

Mr. Obi walked up and shook hands with Mom, Ledward, and Julio's dad.

Then he squatted down and

looked at Darci, eye to eye. "And who are you, young lady?"

Darci looked up at Mom.

"Her name is Darci," I said. "She's my sister."

Mr. Obi studied Darci, his hand cupping his chin. "You want to be in a movie, Darci?"

# 16

# Died Like a Champ

We began filming the next scene, another piece in the puzzle Mr. Obi would put together in his Hollywood studio.

First we watched as they filmed eight men dragging the big steel cages down to the beach.

It turned out that the cages weren't steel at all; they were made of something lighter and painted silver. I probably could have dragged one off the truck by myself. But they looked real, and the actors made them look heavy.

The next scene was Darci's big moment.

Mr. Obi pointed to three adult zombies. "You, you, and you, listen up. I want you to slowly start wandering up toward the homes above the beach. Just when you get close to the houses we're going to blare some music. Zombies are attracted by sound, so when you hear it, you turn away from the neighborhood."

One of the adult zombies raised his hand. "What are those cages for?"

"Those are for a scene we'll film around the time the sun goes down. You'll see. But for now, two things need to happen: One, you head to the houses and turn back when you hear music. Two, you catch this little girl."

Mr. Obi pulled Darci over next to him.

"Benny," he said. "You're going to be the one to catch her. The rest of you will close in and completely surround her . . . and that will be the last we ever see of her."

Shayla gasped. "You mean they *eat* her?"

"A zombie movie has to have drama," Benny said.

Darci grinned. She liked it.

"But that's so mean," Shayla whispered.

Maya touched her shoulder. "It's a movie, Shayla."

"Let's go!" Mr. Obi called.

We headed out.

Lined all along the beach, in the park above, and in people's yards, a huge crowd was watching the filming. Some sat on blankets with kids and ice chests and cameras of their own. Some guys stood like statues with their arms crossed. Windsurfers and kite boarders waited with their gear, giving us looks that said, Hurry it up, already, we want to go in the ocean.

I couldn't blame them.

"Action!"

"Easiest money I ever made," Willy said.

Maya bumped him. "Quiet! What if somebody watching the movie can read lips?"

The three adult zombies broke away and headed toward the houses. When they were almost there, Zumba music blared, and they headed back.

We all turned toward the music.

When it stopped, we went back to our mindless limping.

Waves slapped the shore like always, but when I looked down the beach and saw nothing—no people, no dogs, no kite boarders or windsurfers—it felt really weird. This beach was always hopping with stuff.

Now . . . it felt like the end of the world.

Except for one thing.

There was a little girl wandering toward us. Darci.

Benny groaned and started toward her. The rest of us limped faster, following Benny.

In the story, Darci was some kid walking down the beach not paying attention, just hav-

ing fun splashing through the shallow water. When she looks up, she sees zombies. Man, would that freak me out in real life.

We shuffled faster, making weird noises.

Darci was a good actress. She made like she didn't get what was going on. Just kept on coming down the beach.

When Benny was almost on top of her, she figured it out.

And shrieked!

I gaped. Ho!

It was high and sharp, like a powerful whistle, so clear you could probably hear it all the way over on the other side of the island!

When Benny grabbed her arm she screamed even more, and struggled to get away.

We all closed in.

Benny surrounded her with his arms.

Darci fainted and fell to the sand. I don't think Mr. Obi told her to do that, but it was perfect.

We fell on her.

She died like a champ.

"Cut!"

# 17

# Boom Box

Darci's eyes sparkled when Mr. Obi handed her a crisp fifty-dollar bill and an autographed movie poster of *My Cousin Is a Teenage Vambie.*

"That was brilliant, Darci, just doggone brilliant."

Darci looked up at Mom and smiled.

"For sure, Darce," I said. "You were great."

Julio, Willy, Rubin, Maya, and Shayla all slapped hands with her.

Darci beamed.

Mom pulled her close. "What an exciting day this is."

"Stick around," Mr. Obi said. "More to come."

I elbowed Darci. "Too bad you won't be here to see it, Darce . . . because we just ate you."

"Two more scenes and it's a wrap for the beach," Mr. Obi said. "Gotta go get set up."

He left and I thought, How does he keep everything in his head? There was so much going on.

I asked Benny.

"He's a genius," Benny said. "That, plus he's got Lana. Nothing gets by her."

"Was me," Julio said, "I'd need *five* assistants."

Benny nodded seriously, as if what Julio had said would be true for anyone . . . except him and his uncle, of course. "Wait till you see what we're doing with the cages. Me and my uncle rewrote that scene. It's better now."

We all turned to look at the cages waiting in the trees that lined the beach.

"Really?" I said. "He let you rewrite the script with him?"

"Of course. No big deal. I do it all the time."

Julio shook his head and chuckled. "You are definitely something else, Benny."

Benny shrugged. "Just got it, I guess."

The sun was slipping behind the mountains. Night was coming on, which meant it wouldn't be long before Stella's big moonlight scene.

I looked up. What if there wasn't a moon tonight? I shrugged. This was Hollywood. They could do anything.

Spike Black came over with a suitcase-sized thing on his shoulder. It had big dials on it, like an old radio.

"Spike," Benny said. "These are my friends from the school I used to go to."

Spike smiled, his teeth white as cut coconut. "You guys having fun?"

"For sure," I said. "You're lucky you get to do this all the time."

He laughed. "Not all the time. I do other kinds of movies, too. And I also make guitars. That's my hobby."

"I played a guitar once," Rubin said.

"Cool," Spike said.

"What's that thing on your shoulder?" I asked.

"This," he said, lowering the box, "is an old-time radio called a boom box. It's for the last beach scene."

"Spike is going to use it to draw you away," Benny said. "You'll see."

Later, we all went down onto the beach and did a scene where we limped after Spike with his boom box while the big guys moved the cages down to the sand.

Then Mr. Obi said, "For the last scene I need more to happen than just herding zombies into cages. I need someone else to get caught, but not Spike . . . Spike will save that person."

Mr. Obi looked around at his cast.

"You," he said finally.

Stella lit up.

# 18

# No Escape!

As the sun disappeared behind the mountains that cut across the island, the sky turned from blue to silver, to purple, and finally to black.

The last scene was supposed to be the spookiest of all, and a dark beach shadowed by eerie movie lights would make you think twice about being alone on the sand.

As the night breeze swayed the ironwood trees, Mr. Obi went over the scene with Stella and Spike.

Stella never took her eyes off him. She was one hundred percent focused on her job. She wasn't even Stella anymore, seemed like.

Lana called from the set. "Zombies! Check in with makeup."

Stella's big scene started with all of us back down on the beach, wandering around in the dark. By then we were so tired that when we staggered it was for real. And our groaning turned into something more like snarling and barking.

Then when Spike blasted Zumba music on the boom box, we all turned and growled as we headed toward the noise.

Spike, Stella, and another actor were acting as bait to lure us over to the three huge cages. The idea was that the three of them would break us up into groups and herd us into the cages and lock us up.

Each cage had two doors, one in front and

one in back. The bait would go into the cage and the zombies would follow them. The bait would then escape out the back and slam the door, and the zombies would be locked inside.

That was the plan.

Except Mr. Obi had just rewritten the scene.

It happened like this:

We closed in on the bait, our zombie hunger raging. Julio, Willy, Benny, Rubin, Maya, Shayla, and I headed to the middle cage, our arms out, faces crazy, groaning, barking.

We got closer and closer to the cages.

Stella, Spike, and the other guy taunted us,

coming close, then running back as we limped after them.

The three baits went into the cages.

That would take guts in real life. What if the back door got stuck?

Mr. Obi had thought of that, too, and that was exactly what happened to Stella's escape door.

The other two baits went in and out the back and slammed the cage doors shut and locked the zombies inside them.

Stella's back door wouldn't budge.

She shook it. She beat her fists on it.

She turned around. Zombies were dragging their feet into the cage behind her. She panicked and screamed. Spike and the other guy ran over and tried to get the escape door open.

Stella screamed louder, so loud and so real that I almost stopped being a zombie to watch.

One zombie grabbed her arm. Stella yanked it away. Another came at her from the other side.

Stella fell and four zombies landed on top of her.

At the last second, Spike and the other guy managed to get the door open. They reached in. Spike pulled Stella out while the other guy batted the zombies back with a stick. Stella was scratched, red marks running down her arms and across her face with something the makeup people had given the attacking zombies.

"Lock it!" Spike shouted to the other guy.

He managed to beat the zombies back and slam the cage door and lock it tight.

Spike dragged Stella away. She was sobbing now, tears rolling down her face.

It scared me. It was so *real*.

We moaned louder, reaching our hands through the bars, trying to get to human flesh.

The camera followed as Spike and the other guy carried Stella up to the trees, where Spike had some zombie virus antidote that he invented, because just getting scratched by a zombie was enough to infect you.

He gave Stella a shot.

And Stella blacked out.

"Cut!"

Ho, man.

Nobody said a word. There was only the ocean, lapping up onto the beach.

The scene was over. But all eyes were still on Stella. We wanted to see more.

Finally, Mr. Obi kneeled down and helped her up. Stella rubbed the tears from her face. "Did I do all right?"

"All *right*?" Mr. Obi shook his head. "Young lady, you were amazing! Brilliantly, stunningly, and ferociously amazing."

Stella smiled.

"Let's hear it for Stella!" Mr. Obi said.

The clapping and cheering went on for a full minute.

After we got out of the cages I found Stella and put a hand on her shoulder. "Nice job. I'm not kidding, either."

Stella dabbed at her eye makeup with a tissue. "Thank you."

"Are you crying?"

She shook her head. "It was just . . . intense."

"Yeah, and boy, were you good."

Stella smiled. "Okay, right now you're not a gnome."

"I'll take it."

Shayla came up next to me. "You made me cry, Stella," she said. "I was scared for you."

Stella smiled. "It was hard, but . . . I loved it."

Man oh man oh man, if I live to be a thousand years old I don't think anything will ever be as fun and exciting and weird and awesome as that one long day and night on the beach.

# 19

# Noon in Las Vegas

The next day I got up early. I had a call to make.

It was nine o'clock in Hawaii, so it would be noon in Las Vegas. I hoped he was up.

Dad's wife, Marissa, answered.

"It's me," I said. "Calvin."

"Calvin! Oh, it's so good to hear from you. . . . Is everything all right?"

"Yeah-yeah, everything is fine. I just wanted to talk to . . . to Dad."

"Perfect timing. Hang on, I'll get him. Oh, it's wonderful to hear your voice. I miss you."

"Uh, yeah . . . me too."

I could hear her in the background as she hurried to get Dad. Already I was glad I called. Marissa made me feel good inside.

"Cal?"

"Hi, Dad. Am I . . . um, bothering you?"

"Gee, son, you couldn't bother me in a million years, even if you tried. What's up? Is everything all right?"

I guess that's what

you get when you hardly ever talk to someone on the phone. When you finally do call, they think something's wrong.

But that was changing. Dad and I had talked on the phone twice in the past month already.

"Everything's fine, Dad. I just wanted to tell you that I'm in a movie. And so is Darci, and Stella, too. A zombie one."

"A zombie movie? You mean like a real movie, or is this something one of your friends is making?"

"No, Dad, it's a real one. My friend Benny's uncle is the writer, producer, and director. He's a famous millionaire from Hollywood."

"Hollywood, huh?"

"Yeah, he made that movie called *My Cousin Is a Teenage Vambie.* Did you see it?"

Dad laughed. "Afraid I missed that one, but you know what? I've heard of it. Yeah, I think it passed through town a couple of years ago. Same director, you say?"

"Yeah. He wrote it, too. Me and my friends were extras. We even got paid a hundred dollars!"

"Well, I'll be danged. Getting paid makes you a professional. Did you know that?"

"Did I know what?"

"If you get paid for acting, you can call yourself a professional. That's how it works."

"Ho," I whispered.

"Speaking of money, Calvin, can I say something, man to man?"

"Uh, sure, Dad."

"Marissa and I . . . we opened up two savings accounts. One for you and one for Darci."

"You did?"

"College savings."

"Wow, really? I mean, that's good. I want to go to college."

"That's what we want, too."

Wow. Inside I smiled. Dad was talking to me man to man about *college.* "I won't tell anyone, Dad."

He laughed. "It's not a secret. I told your mom. I just wanted you to know that we all care about your future, Calvin."

"Um . . . thanks."

I didn't know what to say.

"So," Dad went on. "When does this movie come out? I want to see it."

"I don't know, but I'll call you the minute I find out."

"Promise?"

"Yeah, Dad, I promise."

"I'm darn proud of you, son."

"You are?"

"You bet."

We talked a while longer, but my mind was

all over the place. Dad was as excited as I was about what I'd done, and I could feel it, even over the phone.

"Well," I said as we started to run out of things to say. "I guess I'll go down to Julio's house now."

"I remember Julio, and Willy, too. And that nice girl Shayla."

"Uh . . . yeah."

There was a moment of silence.

"Calvin?"

"Yeah, Dad?"

"Thank you for calling me. I am truly, truly happy that you did."

"You are?"

"Yes. I am."

"Yeah, well . . . bye."

"Hey, wait."

"What?"

"Just want to tell you that I love you."

"Uh . . ."

He laughed. "Don't worry. This part will get easier."

"Hunh?"

"Say hi to your friends for me."

"Sure, Dad. See you."

I hung up and just stood there. It was all working out. So what if he lived in Las Vegas and was married to Marissa? At first that had been weird. But now it was . . . okay.

I ran outside with a big smile on my face. I banged on Julio's and Willy's doors.

We had plans.

# 20

## Benny Is Never wrong

Julio was in his backyard playing football . . .
with his *brothers*!

I gaped at them.

Julio saw me and shrugged. "It's not so bad
being a slave sometimes."

He tossed me the ball and four little cock-aroaches charged me. I tossed it back and they turned to follow the ball. "Like a school of fish," I said.

"Marcus," Julio called to the next oldest brother. "Take over for me. I gotta go."

"You got it, bro."

Julio stared at him. "Bro?"

"You say that."

"See?" I said. "They look up to you. You're a star, just like your dad said."

"Let's get out of here."

We took off.

"It's good to have you back again . . . bro," I said as we headed over to grab Willy.

"Pfff!"

After Mr. Obi had wrapped everything up the night before, we'd all gone to my house to celebrate our brand-new fifty-dollar bills. Two each. They smelled good, too. I'd folded mine into small squares and stuffed them into my pocket.

Today me, Julio, and Willy were hoping to

find Benny and his uncle at the beach again. Maybe there was something they'd forgotten to do.

We ran gasping to the park and gazed down on yesterday's sandy zombieland.

"Dang," I said.

It was as if nothing had ever happened there. The beach was back to like it always was on a Sunday morning—runners, dogs, wind-surfers, kite boarders, picnickers, small kids, and sun lovers.

Not one zombie.

Willy tapped my arm and nodded toward the ironwood trees.

Benny was sitting in the shade, his bike lying on the sand next to him.

"What's he doing?" I said.

"Prob'ly thinking about going shark hunt-ing or something. The guy makes stuff up left and right."

"I know," Willy said.

"I think he just does it so people will like him," Julio added.

I frowned. "But we already like him."

"Maybe he doesn't believe it."

"We don't treat him bad," I said.

Julio shrugged. "Just saying."

We headed over.

Benny lifted his chin.

"What you doing?" Julio asked. "Waiting for your uncle? You got more scenes?"

Benny shook his head. "Gone already. Flew back to Hollywood this morning. They'll finish the movie in the studios."

We plopped down around him on the

pinecone-littered sand under the ironwood trees.

"Well, it was fun while it lasted," Willy said. "Thanks for asking us to be in it, Benny."

"No problem."

"Yeah, thanks, Benny." I tossed a pinecone at him. They were the size of marbles, small bullets.

We sat looking out at the ocean glittering with sunlight. No water could ever look better than this, I thought. It made you want to pick it up and wrap it around you like a blanket.

Benny tossed five pinecones at a tree, one after the other. Something was on his mind.

Julio asked, "How come you so . . . like, sad or something?"

It took a few seconds for Benny to answer.

He shrugged. "Maybe you believe this, maybe you don't, but I'm going to miss you guys. I know I'm weird, everybody tells me that. But you didn't care. We had a good time anyway...then I had to go and change schools."

He tossed three more pinecones.

The sound of waves mixed with the shrieks of small kids playing on the beach, a sound that made the day and everything else seem brand-new, like we were starting over.

"Well," I said. "You still live in Kailua, right?"

Benny nodded. "Yeah. Other end of the beach."

"That's not so far. On a bike."

He nodded. "Not that far. I guess."

He must have had new friends from school. But then, maybe not. Kids who went to Iolani came from all over the island. They didn't all live in the same neighborhood like us.

After a long moment, Benny said, "Since I moved here from Hilo, nobody's been nice as you punks. I mean it."

Julio opened his hands. "We're nice guys, what can I say?"

I cracked up.

We got up and headed back toward Kalapawai Market, Benny pushing his bike.

"So," Willy said. "What are you guys going to do with your movie money?"

I thought back to the night before, waving around those fifty-dollar bills. I just sort of wanted to keep them.

But I sort of didn't, too.

"I'm going to buy a new bike," I said. "A bigger one, metallic red or black, with gears. If I have enough."

"My mom took my money," Willy said. "She's going to open a savings account for me."

Julio liked that idea. "Maybe I'll save mine, too."

That made me feel guilty.

Sort of.

"Well, I'm getting a bike."

"I know where you can get a good one," Benny said. "For cheap. A new one would cost more than you have."

"You mean a used bike?"

"More like a rebuilt-to-be-better-than-new bike."

Julio put his hand on my shoulder. "Believe him, Calvin. Is Benny ever wrong?"

I half laughed. "You're right, Julio. He may be weird, but Benny is never wrong."

Even Benny thought that was funny.

# 21

# Old Man Laughing

An hour later, after I'd gone home for my money, Benny packed me on his bike to some mysterious hideaway far different from the Kailua town I knew.

"This place," he said. "It's sort of ... unique."

It was a dump at the end of a bad dirt road.

Not a for-real garbage dump, but a dark shed with rusting junk all over the place. If there was a bike worth buying in that mess it would be a miracle, and I told Benny that.

"Don't be so quick to judge."

We stopped. The place was silent.

Benny dropped his bike. "Follow me."

We picked our way through heaps of old toilets, refrigerators, washing machines, sinks, an old jeep, and boxes of nuts and bolts and screws and everything else you could think of.

"Where'd all this stuff come from?"

"Dump, prob'ly."

Benny stopped just outside the shed. "Hoo-ie," he called into the darkness. "Old man. You home?"

Silence.

Then, *Twang!*

I nearly jumped out of my skin. "Jeese!"

We turned to face a white-haired man holding a large wrench and a garbage can lid. He clanked the lid again and laughed so hard tears came out of his crinkly old eyes.

My heart felt like drums in my chest. Old geezer nearly gave me a heart attack!

"My friend wants a bike with gears," Benny said after the old man settled down. "You got one?"

Still giggling, the old man waved for us to follow him toward the shed.

"Doesn't he talk?" I whispered.

"Only when he needs to."

The old man had a bike, all right. It was sort of silver, with dings and scratches all over it, and even a little rust. He motioned me to it.

"*Norinayo.*"

I looked at Benny. "What'd he say?"

"He wants you to ride it."

"Well, why didn't he say so?"

"He did. He only speaks Japanese."

I frowned at the bike. What a wreck! "Is he serious?"

Benny shrugged. "Take it for a spin. See for yourself."

"Fine."

I rolled the clunker out to the dirt road and looked back toward the shed.

The old man motioned for me to get on it and go.

"Sheese," I mumbled.

I climbed on and rode down the bumpy road, swerving around potholes and rocks . . . and holy bazooks! It was the smoothest, best-handling dang bike I'd ever been on in my whole entire life.

"Wow!"

I rode farther down the road, changed gears, which shifted like silk, then turned around and rode it back. What a bike!

I pulled up in front of Benny and the old man. "How much does he want for it?"

Benny turned to the old man. *"Ikura de-suka?"*

The old man squinted and rubbed his chin. *"Ju doru."*

Benny looked back at me. "Ten dollars."

"Ten? That's *all*? This bike is better than any bike I've ever been on. He only wants *ten*?"

Benny shrugged. "That's what he said. But if I was you, I'd give him a little bit more."

"Why?"

"You said it was a good bike."

"Yeah, but, I'd just be throwing my money away."

"Would you?"

I frowned.

Benny looked around. "The old guy can use it."

That Benny.

I pulled out one of my folded-up fifty-dollar bills and handed it to the old man. "Keep the change."

Benny translated.

When the old man unfolded it his eyes nearly popped out of his head. He stuffed the money in his pocket and broke out laughing.

Benny and I rode away on our bikes doing all the tricks we could think of.

Standing on one pedal.

Riding with our arms out like wings.

Kneeling on the seat.

We even tried sitting backwards . . . but we ended up in somebody's hedge.

"Was a lot of money to that old guy," Benny said. "That was nice of you."

"Your idea."

"Yeah, but it was your money."

"It was a lot, wasn't it?"

Benny nodded. "But look what you did."

I stared at Benny and laughed. I was starting to

feel really good. That old man needed the money. Benny Obi was right again.

"Well," Benny said, slowing to a stop. "My house is that way. Guess I'll see you around . . . sometime."

I hit the brakes and put my feet on the ground.

It was like one of those moments when you're daydreaming and lose track of where you are . . . then you blink and try to remember. "You have to go home?"

He shrugged.

It hadn't even occurred to me that Benny wouldn't spend the rest of the day with me, Julio, and Willy.

"You got chores, or something?"

"I'm writing a screenplay to send to Hollywood. My agent wants . . . wants . . . me to . . ."

"Yeah," I said. "That's cool, Benny."

He glanced behind him. "Well . . ."

I ran my hand over my new bike's rough handlebars. I wanted to tell Benny he didn't have to make up all that stuff about agents and Hollywood. He could just be normal.

But how do you say that to someone?

Benny lifted his chin. "Hey. It was fun doing the movie with you guys. I'll come find you when it's finished. You can have a preview."

I nodded. "Yeah, good."

"Well . . . bye."

He stood on a pedal and headed away, his bike wobbly, then steady.

I couldn't help thinking, Benny had all this big movie stuff going on, and still, he'd come to find us. He never forgot his friends.

"Wait!" I called.

When he slid to a stop and glanced back, the look on his face told me Julio was right. Benny wasn't sure if we liked him, or maybe even if anyone did.

"Forget Hollywood," I said. "Come over. Hang out with us."

"When?"

"Right now, unless you have to–"

"Really?"

I tilted my head. "Really what?"

"I can hang out . . . with you guys?"

"Of *course*. What are you talking about?"

Benny looked at me for a long moment. Then he broke into a smile and pedaled toward me. "Hey, did I ever tell you about the time I trapped a ghost in my bedroom?"

I laughed. "Come on, Benny. You can tell me on the way."

## A Hawaii Fact:

Elvis Presley made three movies in Hawaii: *Blue Hawaii; Girls, Girls, Girls;* and *Paradise, Hawaiian Style.* The islands were his all-time favorite vacation destination.

## A Calvin Fact:

Zombies trip on just about anything in their way. If you put obstacles in their path most of them can't figure it out before tripping.

**Graham Salisbury** is the author of eight other Calvin Coconut books, as well as several novels for older readers, including the award-winning *Lord of the Deep, Blue Skin of the Sea, Under the Blood-Red Sun, Eyes of the Emperor, House of the Red Fish,* and *Night of the Howling Dogs.* Graham Salisbury grew up in Hawaii. Calvin Coconut and his friends attend the same school Graham did—Kailua Elementary School. Graham now lives in Portland, Oregon, with his family. Visit him on the Web at grahamsalisbury.com and CalvinCoconut.com.

 **Jacqueline Rogers** has illustrated more than one hundred books for young readers over the past twenty-five years. She studied illustration at the Rhode Island School of Design. You can visit her at jacquelinerogers.com.